Mother Goose Sails into View

Sunrise, dawn chorus, a long, slim vee
of white winged friends—and one is me.
I honk instructions; we head down
to walk about the sleeping town.

Here, we'll remix old songs anew
to turn them into something true
for modern singers, wingers, readers
to speak aloud at all birdfeeders.

Like soaring eagles, verses flow,
though scribbling with bird feet is slow.
When I sail off at this day's end,
you'll find poems wrought by your bird-brained friend,

xxx

MOTHER GOOSE

Grumbles FROM THE Town

Mother-Goose Voices with a Twist

POEMS BY Jane Yolen AND Rebecca Kai Dotlich

ILLUSTRATIONS BY Angela Matteson

WORDSONG

AN IMPRINT OF HIGHLIGHTS
Honesdale, Pennsylvania

To Caroline and Amelia,
who know their nursery rhymes and love to laugh
—JY

For Bee Cullinan (1926–2015), now among the stars and your
Jonathan, and because this is the only way to say I knew you, I
loved you, I miss you. (You always did love nursery rhymes.)
—RKD

For Mom and Dad, who have always believed
in my artistic ambitions
—AM

The following poems are by Jane Yolen: "Mother Goose Sails into View"; "Shoe Speaks"; "Spinning a Tale"; "I Am the Sock"; "Song of the Vegetarian Princess"; "The Old Dog's Complaint"; "Not Another Fall"; "Plum Tuckered Out"; "Hill Memories"; "A Letter from Fork to His Old Friends"; "The Queen Speaks of the Knave"; "Another Patient Tells Off Dr. Fell"; "The Rosebush Grumbles (Again)"; "Why the Fiddle Is Happy."

The following poems are by Rebecca Kai Dotlich: "Summer in the Shoe"; "Spider Recalls the Tuffet Fright"; "Sleepy John"; "Maid Mutters to Herself"; "Snoring Short Story"; "A Neighbor Gossips to the Gardener about the Humpty Brothers"; "Brother Spy"; "The Pail's Take on It"; "Spoon Says"; "The Knave of Tarts"; "Letter from a Young Patient"; "Little Bird, from a Branch"; "The King's Daughter Remembers"; "Mother Goose Calls Good-bye."

The following poem is by both authors: "Mouse Adventures: A Poem for Three Voices."

WordSong
An Imprint of Highlights
815 Church Street
Honesdale, Pennsylvania 18431
Printed in China

ISBN: 978-1-59078-922-3
Library of Congress Control Number: 2015958504

First edition
Designed by Anahid Hamparian
Production by Sue Cole
The text of this book is set in Quicksand.
The illustrations were done in acrylic and colored pencil on wood board.
10 9 8 7 6 5 4 3 2 1

For Our Dear Readers:

Nursery rhymes from around the world are, among other things, a mix of lullabies, street rhymes, weather rhymes, and riddles, sprinkled with playful puns and a nod to long ago times.

We have selected fourteen of them, some famous Mother Goose rhymes and some special favorites of ours and our own children and grandchildren. We've reinvented them in two different voices, playing with points of view. So, we rhymed the old woman who lives in the shoe from the viewpoint of the shoe itself, spun our own webs as the spider tells of meeting Miss Muffet, became the plum as he shouts in bouncing lines his anger at Little Jack Horner, and more.

We chose fourteen poems. But if you read a book of Mother Goose rhymes, you'll find a hundred more you might like to play with in your own poems. Maybe have the hill give advice to the Noble Duke of York. Or perhaps tell us why the hickory dickory clock is laughing as the mice race up its sides. Or maybe where the horse goes after it trot, trot, trots to Boston.

Write a funny poem or a serious one. Use your own imagination to create magic. Enjoy the joy.

—Jane and Rebecca

contents

Shoe Speaks

I love the sound of giggles
from the lace-swings in the tree,
the thump of running feet
as children race on home to me.

But best is how I love them
when they dream inside my toe.
Do you doubt a shoe can love?
I have a sole, you know.

Shoe

Summer in the Shoe

It was *so* hot, living in leather
all day and all night. Sunlight
spilled through the open top,
tumbled down stairs,
rested on the cat.
Imagine this, imagine that . . .
read books in a heel,
ate supper in a toe.
Blew bubbles
from small windows,
rolled marbles down the tongue,
bump, bumpity, bump.
Played next door
in a pirate ship—
lots of space to roam.
Still, we liked going home.

9

Little Miss Muffet

Spinning a Tale

She didn't like tuffet,
she didn't like lines.
She complained of my gossamer web
where it shines.

She didn't like whey
that I brought for a treat.
She said that a spider
has too many feet.

She was nasty and naughty.
I gave her a push.
And instead of the tuffet,
her tush met a bush.

Spider Recalls the Tuffet Fright

So there I was,
dangling and spinning
like spiders do,
minding my own business,
watching her chew
curdles and clumps
below my trapeze.
*What is **that**?* I asked
(in my best spider*eeze*)—
Achoo!
    I sneezed.
She whooped.
She wailed.
Shouted "GESUNDHEIT!"
and bailed.

DIDDLE, DIDDLE, DUMPLING, MY SON JOHN

SLEEPY JOHN

Diddle, diddle, dumpling,
dumpling, diddle, John—
one shoe off, both socks on.
One shoe missing in the night;
is it the left, or is it the right?
He's counting shoes instead of sheep,
when all he wants to do is sleep.
One shoe gone (a sleepy score).
Diddle, diddle, dumpling.
Snore, John, snore.

I Am the Sock

I am the sock,
all black and blue
from too much use.
And when he's through,
he throws me out,
no wash, no rinse.
Does Dumpling John
think he's a prince?

But joke's on him—
this story ends,
me all awash
with brand-new friends.
My pals are colorful,
sturdy fliers,
who've fled the evil
of the dryers.

So rise, you socks,
and heed my call:
dump Dumpling Johns
for once and all.
Live free of dryers,
free of pain,
just wash and rinse
yourself in rain.

And never fit
a foot again.

Sing a Song of Sixpence

Song of the Vegetarian Princess

Sing a song of salad,
a pocket full of beans,
four-and-twenty cantaloupes
stashed inside my jeans.

Will I eat some blackbirds
baked into a pie?
No, I'd rather see them all
flying in the sky.

14

Maid Mutters to Herself

I was hanging sheets on the line
when birds attacked.
Insane! It began to rain
a downpour of **blackbirds**!
A bloke poked his head out the window.
King wants another pie! he cried.
I mumbled a few choice words, I did.
Who, I ask you, in their right mind
bakes pies of *birds*?
I stomped and shooed
them all away.
Black*berries* make sweeter pies
any day.

It's Raining, It's Pouring

The OLD Dog's complaint

It's raining, it's pouring,
and *everyone* is snoring.

Despite some cotton
in each ear,
the only sound
that I can hear
is snore-snore-snore
and snore some more
coming straight at me
through the doghouse door.

It's so dang loud,
I cannot think.
I cannot dream
or sleep a wink.
I much prefer
the drip-drop rain.
No wonder, then,
this sad refrain:

It's raining, it's pouring,
and *everyone* is snoring.
   (Except for me!)

Snoring Short Story

Yes, yes, yes, I snore.
Long, loud, goose-gurgling snores.
Usually when it rains.
Especially when it pours,
I snores.

17

HUMPTY DUMPTY

NOT ANOTHER FALL

Humpty Dumpty
skates on a wall,
another big tumble,
another pratfall.
Another big grin
when he jumps to his feet.
He's got loads of jokes
that just cannot be beat.
He's our class clown;
that's never in doubt,
but that's why he's sitting
again
in time-out.

A Neighbor Gossips to the Gardener about the Humpty Brothers

Here's what I heard:

SPLAT!

Said to myself, *what was that?*
A Humpty had fallen
to the other side.
He was roundish,
and small. Fell from the wall.
Always in places
they shouldn't be.
Then the *other one* tumbled
from an apple tree.
News came in twos: a cut and a bruise.
(Lucky they didn't break any legs.)
Those Humpty boys
are mischievous eggs.

19

Little Jack Horner

Brother Spy

Ruined! One perfect plum.
Spoiled by a germy thumb.
And I had my eye on that pie.
OK, no one likes a snoop.
But Jack demolished it.
Created a pie-typhoon.
So toss the fork—I'll need a spoon!

PLUM TUCKERED OUT

Here it comes—
another thumb.
Is that the way
to treat a plum?
I grew gentle
on the tree.
Sun and rain
were good to me.

But now there's heat
and boyish laughter.
What horrors might be
coming after?
Go away, hand,
don't be dumb.
Don't you dare poke *me*
with that thumb.

Jack and Jill Went Up the Hill

Hill Memories

I remember ice,
I remember chill,
I remember climbers,
I remember spill,
I remember tumble,
and voices shrill.

I remember Jack.
I remember Jill.

22

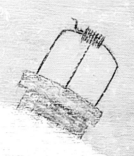

The Pail's Take on It

They trudged their way
up to the town's bubbly.
Step after step.
Two by two.
Jill and Jack, Jack and Jill.
Up, up, up that hill.
And there was *me*, swinging
from a thin, tin handle:
back and forth, back and forth.
Boom! Jack tripped on Jill.
Both tumbled down that hill.
And I, the pail,
went handle over tail.
What did they do?
Jack and Jill, Jill and Jack.
They both got up—went right back,
filled me up with cold, fresh water.
I was thirsty that day.
Good kids, I say.

HEY DIDDLE DIDDLE

A Letter from Fork to His Old Friends

Cat's got the fiddle,
cow's got the moon,
laughing dog sings
that same silly tune.
Dish has the best, though:
he's married my spoon.

You ran far away,
and left me alone.
Not a one of you writes,
or picks up a phone.
All is forgiven, folks.
Please, please, come home.

Signed, your old friend Fork

spoon says

I'm so glad Dish picked me.
I was hoping so.
It was crazy up there,
what with all the fiddles
and cows and cats.
It was too much, I tell you.
Sure, dog laughed.
He had a wacky sense of humor.
Although in truth, he was jealous
of cat, hated playing second fiddle.
And so you have it.
Dish whisked me away from it all.
Sometimes I still dream
in *meow* and *moo*,
imagining only stars and air . . .
where no one notices
an unlikely pair.

The Queen of Hearts

The Queen Speaks of the Knave

I met him first at school.
He sang the latest songs,
knew every lyric.
And jokes?
He was hysterical,
a real stand-up guy,
a card who always
had us in stitches.

The teachers, those witches,
couldn't stand him,
though if that hurt Knave,
it didn't show.
But me—
I'd already given him my heart.
Why not a tart?

The Knave of Tarts

He longed to marry a wife who had perfected the tart.
When a lovely girl finally offered her heart, she said:
My hours are spent with books on my shelf.
So if you want tarts, you'll make them yourself.

He now owns a tart shop in the town of Reed.
And he keeps very, very busy indeed.

27

I Do Not Like Thee, Doctor Fell
Letter from a young patient

Dear Doctor Fell,

I'd like you better (for sure) if you gave out jars of jelly beans.

Or parakeets! Candy lips. Sticky eyes and licorice.

Bags of rubber spiders. Windup frogs. Goldfish.

My best advice? Think twice. About the shot.

Then I'd *really* like you.

A lot.

Truly,

Julie

Age 7

Another Patient Tells Off Dr. Fell

I do not like you, Doctor Fell.
You didn't warm your hands real well.
You cleared your throat too near my ear,
then wondered why I couldn't hear.
Your breath was stinky as blue cheese.
You banged a hammer on my knees.
You didn't say to look away
before that shot I got today.
You chuckled when I cried a bit,
and made me feel the perfect twit.

No—
I do not like you, Dr. Fell,
but this I know, and this I tell
to anyone but you, old Fell:
I like you . . .

       when you make me well.

29

Ring Around the Rosie

The Rosebush Grumbles (Again)

Every day it is the same:

the children play the Rosie game.

They dance around me in a ring

and then begin to chant and sing.

It's much too loud, my roots get sore,

and still they sing and dance some more.

My stems grow thorny; petals fall.

I do not like their song at all.

It's simply such a boring sound,

I wish that they would all *stay* down.

(Grumble, mumble, fumble, yawn,

I wish they'd just get off my lawn!)

Little Bird, from a Branch

Wish I could hold hands too,
play their circle game, sing
ashes, ashes,
but I just toddle and tweet
on my knotty branch,
pitter-pat back and forth
back and forth,
squeeze little bird eyes,
listen to *we all fall down.*
I peek at heads, as the circlers
go chanting *ashes, ashes;*
it begins to rain
as they *all fall down*
in a rosebush chain.

OLD KING COLE

The King's Daughter Remembers

He was always losing his pipe.
The game was who could find it first.
Getting to pick the next song was our prize.
I loved his eyes. They twinkled as he played
that fiddle from morning till night.
We danced from room to room, stayed up late.
He chanted a song: "Clock hands can wait!"
He sang to the servants:
"Bring cherries and cheeses!
Bring chocolates and creams!"
I hear that fiddle in my dreams.

Why the Fiddle is Happy

He was King Karaoke,
with old songs and new,
and even the queen
got to warble a few.
The court loved that game,
singing till it grew light.
And I got to play
through the long, tuneful night.

33

Three Blind Mice
Mouse Adventures: A Poem for Three Voices

You think you know the rhyme?
You might.
But hear me out.
We were not blind,
just near of sight.
We wore thick glasses
day and night.

We'd left the farm in quite a hurry.

You know us mice—*scurry, scurry.*

One step ahead
of trap or cat.

(Imagine that.)

So we found a town, a store.

An aisle, some cheeses.

(The kind of day that pleases
a mouse.)

Don't cut me off.

A joke, a poke, a pun, a slice of fun.

The Original Nursery Rhymes

There was an Old Woman Who Lived in a Shoe

There was an old woman who lived in a shoe.
She had so many children she didn't know what to do!
So she gave them some broth without any bread,
And she whipped them all soundly and sent them to bed!

Sing a Song of Sixpence

Sing a song of sixpence, a pocket full of rye,
Four-and-twenty blackbirds baked in a pie.
When the pie was opened, the birds began to sing,
Oh, wasn't that a dainty dish to set before the king?

The king was in his counting house counting out his money,
The queen was in the parlor eating bread and honey,
The maid was in the garden hanging out the clothes,
When down came a blackbird and pecked off her nose!

Diddle, Diddle, Dumpling, My Son John

Diddle, diddle, dumpling, my son John,
Went to bed with his trousers on;
One shoe off, and one shoe on,
Diddle, diddle, dumpling, my son John!

Jack and Jill Went Up the Hill

Jack and Jill went up the hill to fetch a pail of water.
Jack fell down and broke his crown
And Jill came tumbling after.
Up got Jack, and home did trot
As fast as he could caper
He went to bed and bound his head
With vinegar and brown paper.

Humpty Dumpty

Humpty Dumpty sat on a wall,
Humpty Dumpty had a great fall.
All the King's horses and all the King's men
Couldn't put Humpty together again.

Little Miss Muffet

Little Miss Muffet sat on a tuffet
Eating her curds and whey.
Along came a spider,
Who sat down beside her
And frightened Miss Muffet away.

It's Raining, It's Pouring

It's raining, it's pouring,
The old man is snoring.
He went to bed and he bumped his head
And couldn't get up in the morning.

Little Jack Horner

Little Jack Horner
Sat in a corner
Eating his Christmas pie.
He put in his thumb,
And pulled out a plum,
And said, "What a good boy am I!"

Hey Diddle Diddle

Hey diddle diddle, the cat and the fiddle,
The cow jumped over the moon.
The little dog laughed to see such fun
And the dish ran away with the spoon!

The Queen of Hearts

The Queen of Hearts,
She made some tarts,
All on a summer's day;
The Knave of Hearts,
He stole those tarts,
And took them clean away.
The King of Hearts
Called for the tarts,
And beat the knave full sore;
The Knave of Hearts
Brought back the tarts,
And vowed he'd steal no more.

Old King Cole

Old King Cole was a merry old soul, and a merry old soul was he;
He called for his pipe and called for his bowl,
And he called for his fiddlers three.
Every fiddler had a fine fiddle, and a very fine fiddle had he;
Oh, there's none so rare as can compare
With King Cole and his fiddlers three.

Three Blind Mice

Three blind mice, three blind mice.
See how they run, see how they run.
They all ran after the farmer's wife,
Who cut off their tails with a carving knife.
Did you ever see such a sight in your life
As three blind mice?

Ring Around the Rosie

AMERICAN VERSION:
Ring-a-round the rosie,
A pocket full of posies,
Ashes! Ashes!
We all fall down.

BRITISH VERSION:
Ring-a-ring o' roses,
A pocket full of posies,
A-tishoo! A-tishoo!
We all fall down.

I Do Not Like Thee, Dr. Fell

I do not like thee, Doctor Fell,
The reason why I cannot tell;
But this I know, and know full well,
I do not like thee, Doctor Fell.

About the Original Nursery Rhymes

There Was an Old Woman Who Lived in a Shoe

This English nursery rhyme goes back to at least the eighteenth century, and is thought by some to be about either Queen Caroline, who had eight children, or her husband King George II, who introduced the fashion of men wearing long white wigs and was nicknamed "The Old Woman."

Little Miss Muffet

Entomologist Dr. Thomas Muffet, author of the first scientific catalog of British insects, had a daughter named Patience, who was supposedly frightened by one of his spiders while having breakfast. This rhyme may be based on this incident, or it may refer to Catholic Mary Queen of Scots, the spider being her enemy, the Protestant preacher John Knox.

Diddle, Diddle, Dumpling, My Son John

No one seems to know where this rhyme came from, but "Diddle, diddle, dumpling," is what peddlers of hot dumplings on London streets used to cry out while selling their scrumptious treats.

Sing a Song of Sixpence

In the Middle Ages in Europe, cooks regularly baked blackbirds and other songbirds in pies. An Italian cookbook from 1549 mentions live birds in a pie. As either a joke or for a special celebration, the cook put birds (often pigeons) in between baked crusts, and when the pie was cut open, they flew out.

It's Raining, It's Pouring

This is yet another nursery rhyme with little history, though some scholars have suggested that it's English because of the amount of rain that falls in Britain, and some have suggested that it's Irish.

Humpty Dumpty

Although the phrase "Humpty Dumpty" held varied meanings in different time periods, it was also the name of a cannon used in England's Civil War in 1648. It sat on the roof of St. Mary's Church. When the church was blown up by the enemy, down fell Humpty Dumpty, too broken to be put together again. Illustrator John Tenniel was the first person to portray Humpty Dumpty as an egg, in Lewis Carroll's *Through the Looking-Glass and What Alice Found There*.

Little Jack Horner

Many say this rhyme mocks the Bishop of Glastonbury who is rumored to have sent the king a bribe to leave his abbey alone—the deeds to twelve great houses baked in a pie. The bishop's steward, Jack (or Thomas) Horner, stuck his finger into the pie and pulled out a real plum—the deed to the great manor house of Mells, which remained in the Horner family's possession until the twentieth century.

Jack and Jill Went Up the Hill

This rhyme has sometimes been considered to be about King Louis XVI of France, who was beheaded (lost his crown), and Queen Marie Antoinette, also beheaded (tumbled) after him in 1793 in the French Revolution. However, the rhyme was published before these deaths occurred, so that's not likely the real meaning behind the verse. In the nineteenth century (when the rhyme got its happier ending), brown paper soaked in vinegar was thought to heal bruises.

Hey Diddle Diddle

While the "Hey diddle diddle," refrain is mentioned in Shakespeare, the full rhyme was not published anywhere until 1765 and Shakespeare died in 1616. Its history is unclear; it seems to be simply a whimsical, nonsense rhyme for children.

The Queen of Hearts

These characters are based on playing cards. The rhyme was first published with three other stanzas—"The King of Clubs," "The King of Spades," and "The Diamond King"—in 1782 in the popular British publication, *The European Magazine,* although "The Queen of Hearts" was well known before then.

I Do Not Like Thee, Dr. Fell

Believed to be written by English poet Tom Brown in the seventeenth century, this poem is not about a medical doctor, but about Dr. John Fell, a professor and dean of Christ Church College at Oxford University who expelled the student Tom Brown. It's said, in retaliation, Brown wrote the rhyme.

Ring Around the Rosie

This popular rhyme was first published in 1881, but nursery rhyme scholars have found references to it that go back much further. For a long time, researchers thought it was about the Bubonic Plague in Europe, but most scholars no longer believe this.

Old King Cole

There were three Celtic kings of Britain named Coel (in English, Cole) in the third to fifth centuries, and no one knows with assurance which one this rhyme celebrates, if any of them.

Three Blind Mice

This song has existed since the seventeenth century, but wasn't published in a children's version until 1842. Possibly, it's about another queen—Bloody Mary Tudor, daughter of Henry VIII, who was known as "the farmer's wife" because of all the land she and her absentee husband, King Philip of Spain, owned. Scholars suggest the three blind mice may be three Protestant noblemen she did away with because of their religion.

Mother Goose Calls Good-Bye

It's time I flew off these pages,
flutter my feathers like sails.
I leave you wild goose tales,
small chimes, a whimsy of rhymes.
They will ring in your ears,
through the town,
through the years.
They will spin again
       and again, like a song.
                    So long!
Trace my shadow on the moon.
See you soon,

    xxxMG